35176519 3/07

Swing High, Swing Low

A Book of Opposites

written by Fiona Coward
illustrated by Giovanni Manna

Barefoot Books
Celebrating Art and Story

Up the ladder,
down the stairs.

Under the table,
over the chairs.

Tummy says "yes,"
   Mommy says "no."

Red says stop.
Green says go.

White is light,
black is dark.

Run to the gate,
walk through the park.

Puddles are wet,
feet are dry.

Swing low to the ground,
then high in the sky.

A time to work,
and a time to play.

Mess it all up,
then tidy away.

Joe makes me laugh,
Kate makes me cry.

Call "hello,"
and wave "good-bye."

The sun is hot,
    ice cream is cold.

Babies are young,
grandparents are old.

Whisper a secret,
try not to shout.

Bring in the laundry,
put the cat out.

Pull up the covers,
    roll down the sheet.

The moon is awake,
but the house is asleep.

For my daughters, Erin and Megan — F. C.
A Miriam, per i suoi preziosi consigli — G. M.

Barefoot Books
2067 Massachusetts Ave
Cambridge MA, 02140

This book was typeset in Infant Calligraphic Bold 30pt
The illustrations were prepared in china ink and watercolor on watercolor paper

Graphic design by Nicky Jex, Henley-on-Thames
Color separation by Bright Arts, Singapore
Printed and bound in Hong Kong by South China Printing

This book has been printed on 100% acid-free paper

Libary of Congress Cataloging-in-Publication Data

Coward, Fiona.
    Swing high, swing low : a day of opposites / written by Fiona Coward ; illustrated by Giovanni Manna.
        p. cm.
    Summary: As they enjoy a busy day, a mother and two children encounter an abundance of contrasts, such as playing and working, laughing and crying,
and waking and sleeping.
ISBN 1-84148-170-X (alk. paper)
    [1. English language--Synonyms and antonyms--Fiction.2. Day--Fiction 3. Stories in rhyme.] Manna, Giovanni, 1966-ill.II. Title.
PZ8.3.C8339Sw 2005
[E]--dc22

2004017714

1 3 5 7 9 8 6 4 2

Barefoot Books
Celebrating Art and Story